Anne Gardner Hale

Folly's bells

A German legend

Anne Gardner Hale

Folly's bells
A German legend

ISBN/EAN: 9783337154615

Printed in Europe, USA, Canada, Australia, Japan

Cover: Foto ©Andreas Hilbeck / pixelio.de

More available books at **www.hansebooks.com**

*Y*E who mid the Christmas cheer
   Fain would linger long
Joyous minstrelsy to hear,
   Careless jest and song,

Marvel not, if, follows mirth —
   From its radiance wrought —
Down the doleful slopes of earth,
   Shadowy afterthought.

Heartsome, wholesome, else, were not
   Merry Christmas ways,
And the lesson soon forgot
   Of these happy days.

Prelude

High o'er the city's din,
The old church bell, by touch impetuous rung,
Threw on the frosty air a vigorous peal,
Which at much hazard set the ancient tower,
That throbbed and swayed all tremulous from its force,
While to the ear expectant came its tones
Sweetest of sounds upon this hallowed eve.
Within the sacred walls, the living green
Of pungent pine and faithful hemlock lent
Symbolic teaching to the chanting choir,
Where all the lights ablaze more joyous made
The blessed service for this festal hour.
Without, the evening star beamed softly forth,
As might of old the star o'er Bethlehem's plains;
Through conquered clouds the full moon cast her rays
Of tenderest glory on the snow-capped roofs,
And silvered all the dingy courts and streets.
There, hurrying to and fro, went busy throngs
Intent on Christmas traffic or its mirth

(Gift-laden most, yet giftless want passed too),
Jostling each other in good-natured strife
For precedence of place or time, with glee
Of gladsome smiles and quiet glance that told,
More plainly far than words, of joy serene.

Just on the edge of trade—scarce counted in—
A modest mansion stood.   Along its front
The snow untrodden and unsullied lay.
Among the crowd, a pale boy, poorly clad,
Espied the snow and ran with eager speed
To reach the entrance, natural shyness gone.
The parlor windows are alight, yet not
For this he comes, nor for the Christmas tree
(So dear to childhood's heart) revealed therein,
Sparkling with tapers and its tinseled gauds
And gifts of gorgeous hues.   He heeds them not,
Nor yet the graceful figures, young and fair,
Swaying and bending gaily in the dance
To music's witching spell.   No—not to these
Gives even a glance; and one, observant, calls
From upraised sash to know his quest, his want.

"Work, work," he utters piteously. "The snow

To clear from doorstep and from court. Work—work!
My mother, sister May, and I, no food
For two long days have tasted, and to earn
Money to buy us bread I'll do my best."

    Impatient children open wide the door
And draw reluctantly the boy within;
All proud and eager to display and share
With him the toys and lavish dainties spread
To make the festival.

                " No, no!" he cries;
With spurning hands and tearful eyes returns
The pretty baubles, and the sweetmeats too.
"I want not these.   Our precious baby May
Moans in her hungry sleep, and mother weeps
That she for lack of bread must die.   Bread—bread!
If but a crust, I'll take it gratefully,—
Yet not as gift.   I can work, and I will,
To pay for all we want."

                Straightway assured
Of this, industriously he plies his task,
And soon with smiling face the needed food

Takes home; while mimic Santa Claus,
With jingling bells and thud of hoof-beats heard
Around the house, comes in and spreads his pack,
Dealing to all assembled for the feast,
In sweet remembrance of the Gift divine
Sent down from heaven on this auspicious eve,
Affection's gifts of whatsoever most
Appropriate are or ardently desired.

To one amid that company he gives
A slender book, wherein is written small,
In the quaint style of ancient days,
A wondrous legend still believed for truth.
She pores the pages with a greedy eye,
And in her memory lingers long the tale,
Whose import deep at length she clearly grasps,
And yearning then to lend its teachings high
To souls congenial, with more ample lines,
In words familiar and of modern guise,
Here upon these fair leaves 'tis spread to view.

Folly's Bells

Folly's Bells

I

When the calm waters of the Zuyder Zee
Ebb slowly out to meet the sleeping sea,—
  What time, o'erwearied, fierce Euroclydon,
    In the far caverns of the icy north,
  Dreaming of contests won,
    Forgets his goings forth,—
The home-bound sailor's gleeful shout is stilled,
His heart with horror chilled;
For there, beneath the waves serene,
Smit with a ghastly splendor through the green,
He sees a city dead — the towers and domes
Of ancient Stavoren, once happy homes,—
A wan eidolon now, the refluent sea
  In these brief moments of complacent mien
From its long dole of darkness setting free—
  Like as from dungeon a dethronèd queen.

Folly's Bells

II

O Stavoren ! fair Stavoren !
Erst among noblest of the marts of trade ;
By wealth and pomp so graced !
How humbled ! how abased !
And to this doom betrayed
By a weak Friesian dame,
Who, blindly arrogant,
Mocked at all pain and want,
Perversely reckless of the sin and shame,
If but her vanity
Might hold supremacy.
And to her sumptuous courts came embassies,
A giddy, thriftless throng,
Sent from all realms, with fulsome flatteries
Joining her dowried minstrels in their song,
Crying in blatant tones that her alone
Empress of splendor all the world should own.
Thus sped long, prosperous years.
Fearless of adverse skies,
With sunny brow, and eyes
As yet undimmed by tears,

From her fine windows far and wide looked she —
  That haughty dame Richberta — many a day
Watching with pride the white sails, fleet and free,
  Fluttering outward from Stavoren bay,
Or the home-coming keel, with treasures vast
Deep-laden, dip lowly the bending mast.

III

Ships the staunchest were hers to run
  Swift as a shuttle to and fro
Every kingdom under the sun —
  Weaving a web of friendship so,

And of the bounty that blesses earth —
  Wealth of the seas or worth of the land,
Or whatsoever therein had birth,
  Readily bringing at her command ;

While timber and granite from Noroway,
  And iron and copper from Russian mines,
Higher and broader day by day
  Builded her towers or lengthened her lines.

Then cedar and cinnabar, silver and gold,
　　Velvet and satin and finest wool,
In plinth and pillar, and fold on fold,
　　Yielded their beauty to her control.

And hosts of ministrants — deftest — best —
　　Wrought with a tireless brain and hand, *
Or waited, obsequient, every guest,
　　And spread her praises throughout the land.

IV

With all this pomp elate,
The porter at Richberta's palace gate
　　Welcomed one merry Christmas morn
A gray-haired man, who leant
Upon an oaken staff.　Wrinkled and bent
Was he,— o'erburdened with the many cares
Which he had gathered unawares
　　From the sad hearts to want and sorrow born,
　　That, out of poverty and pain forlorn,
　　　Had dropped full heavily
　　　Into the bundle of his patient life

"A gray-haired man, who leant upon an oaken staff."   P. 10.

Woes which eye cannot see
Nor will the ear attend amid the strife
When selfish aims and avarice compete
Where wealth and grandeur have their lofty seat.

V

Lackeys and menials base cast many a stare,
And mutter many a sneer
Upon the gray-haired pilgrim drawing near,
Whose calm, clear eyes of eager scrutiny
Pierce through and through
All things within his view,
Behold the glitter and the specious glare
Of all this lavish splendor silently ;
Beauty and grace of varied forms and hues
Nor dazzle nor confuse
His earnest gaze.   With footsteps firm he treads
Where'er the outer court its show dispreads.

VI

The inner court — the gorgeous banquet-hall !
Here the slant sunbeams fall

O'er crowded buffet and on loaded board.
All costly wines are poured,
And luscious viands in profuse display —
Meats, fruits, and comfits — make a grand array
In golden vessels radiant as the morn
   That breaks o'er summer seas in majesty.
Beakers and goblets that rich gems adorn,
   Salvers and chargers crusted preciously
With opulence of jewels ; patterned rare —
Moorish, or arabesque,— all quaintly fair,
Challenge attention — claim, as homage due,
Warm admiration—and receive it, too,
Save from that pilgrim gray,
Who searches o'er and o'er the vast display,
And with a saddened visage turns away.

VII

High on her dais, in regal state,
   Lady Richberta surveys the scene ;
Fawning courtiers may kneel and wait
   While she studies the old man's mien.

Soon, at her mandate, a trumpet brays ;
  He heeds the signal, he stands at her feet,
And shimmer of satin and diamonds' blaze
  The tattered serge of his mantle meet.

He bows on his staff, but he bends not knee,
  Though he notes the ire in her scintillant eyes,
And, as Bragi might answer fierce Atè,
  To her anxious questioning thus replies :

"Most gracious lady, having heard the fame
Of your great wealth and loveliness, I came,
Leaving the old Hercynian woods, whose shade
    Shelters my hut of clay,
  And my pale brothers, in their poverty,
    Far, far behind.
  I crossed the foaming sea,
  Of every mortal evil unafraid,
    If, haply, I might find
    Amid your grand array
The one best thing all-wise, all-potent Heaven
To this bright world hath given.

"Vain is my quest.
Amid your glittering stores I find it not,
  O lady proud and gay!
Your mirthful life is but a wretched lot;
    With that unblest,
  Empty as dross is all this proud array;
Your wealth, a dewdrop in the summer's sun;
Your claim to highest splendor, falsely won."

VIII

At these plain words
  Baffled ambition and chagrin intense
Their balefires mounted on Richberta's cheek.
  Thrice she essayed to speak,
But, held in leash by passion's furious power,
    Her tongue and lips refuse
  Their wonted office. Yet her virulence
    Of gesture swift imbues
Her minions with her ire. Their black brows lower,
    And, drawing ready swords,

With angry menacing of fearful fate
They speed the old man to the city's gate.

     Then through the scurrile crowd
Of pampered flatterers feasting at her board
     Uprose the wassail loud ;
Full freely flowed the mead, red wine was poured ;
     And ribaldry
     In song and glee
Started strange echoes 'neath the tapestries ;
  Smote the still evening air, whose tranquil wings,
  As of a grievèd spirit's murmurings,
Filled all the starry spaces with its sighs.

IX

Ere the next noon, through every house and hut
The rumor passed that Heinric Schleyversen,
The boldest admiral of all her fleet,
Obedient to the mandate first promulged
At dawn by Korthar, privy counselor
And trusted friend of Lady Richberta,
Had summoned all his mariners in haste,

And quay and dock swarmed with a motley crowd
That bustled to and fro in eager zeal.

Where the great ships lay idly moored arose
The quick, sharp strokes of hurrying artisans,
The heavy thud of sledge and adze, the clank
Of chains, the creak of windlass, and the twang
Of loosened cordage, with the rustling, shrill
And sibilant, of unbrailed canvas.   Thus
Through labor's mighty diapason rang
The grandest anthem earth can raise to heaven.

Hard hands of toil, bronzed brows, and sinewy
        arms,
Yours was the grandeur, yours the nobleness,
That had Atlantean splendor gladly brought
Misguided Richberta, were that her wish!

X

Heinric Schleyversen stroked his yellow beard,
And, with the air of one who holds secure
A weighty secret, trod with conscious power
His vessel's deck and gave in bugle tones

His orders right and left, till all the fleet,
Made stanch and burnished as for festival,
Passed down the bay one quiet, starry eve
When tides propitious bore them safely forth
And gracious breezes filled the swelling sails.
　Lady Richberta, in her queenliest robes,
Surrounded by her maids, looked from her tower.
Cresset and torch alight their fullest beams
Flinging athwart the jewels in her hair,
Most beauteous beacon of the night she stood,
Which the departing fleet beheld in awe,
Chivalric likening, with irreverent breath,
To some pure saint with heavenly nimbus crowned.
　Thus watched she there till every snowy sail
Dipped low beneath the far horizon's rim,
Her lords in waiting wondering at her stay.
Yet none durst break the silence of the hour
Nor ask the purport of the whispered words
That stirred her pallid lips as she at length,
All tremulous, came down the marble stairs
And hastened on to reach the banquet hall.

XI

Then, with a frenzy wild, she loudly called
    Her minstrel band,
    And gave a stern command—
In accents that appalled
    By their sepulchral sound
    The sycophants around—
That mirth and merriment should speed apace
    The slowly passing hours,
    And with a ghastly face
And air distraught evoked the highest powers
    Of dulcimer and flute,—
That might allay the tumult in her soul,
    Her saddest fears confute,
Her dark forebodings banish or control.

XII

So passed the feverish days —
    Her greed, insatiate,
Seeking many, many ways
    To draw within the palace gate

All novelties and wonders yet ungained,
If, peradventure, thus might be obtained
  The one best thing
  That should true splendor bring.
For this with wasting envy now she pined,—
The hoary pilgrim's words still fresh in mind.
Yet fruitless all her care, and all the skill
By which her servitors would fain fulfill
  Her wildest scheme.

  Months flee — yet all in vain
  Is effort and appeal to gain
  The treasure craved so long.
And even its search seems but a senseless dream
 To those who stroll her glittering corridors,
 With vaunting voice count her increasing stores,
And lead the dance and troll the fulsome song.

XIII

The years move slowly on. In discontent,
Yet haunted by the hope of gaining soon
  That one best thing,

Lady Richberta keeps, with strictest care,
Whene'er the new moon from her silver shell
Showers softest radiance over Flevum's tide,
A vigil, vowed in secret that fair night
When Heinric Schleyversen sailed down the bay;
Vigil of penance and petition wild,
That this her heart's desire may be obtained.
   Through seven long years — oh! weary, waiting
      years!
No answer had she to her earnest prayers:
Yet through those years she failed not in her vow,
. But climbed religiously the long, steep stairs
Within the watchtower to its highest floor,
Just as each new moon flung a parting ray
Along the river's breast, and Hesperus
With radiant fingers locked the gates of day;
And till the hour of midnight, on her knees,
Her straining eyes sought painfully the bay,
Yearning for signs of the returning fleet.
Then, until dawn, in sleepless agony,
Perversely blind to other needs, her soul,
With tearful voice, in prayer importunate

Besieged Heaven's courts for that most precious boon,
      The one best thing,
To crown the cup, which, for her craving thirst
Of power and splendor, most egregiously,
Had base ambition, with consummate art,
Filled to the jeweled brim.
      Thus, thus she watched,
And prayed, and wept, with superstitious zeal
For the completion of her selfish will,
Nor heeded how, outside her palace-walls,
Famine, disease, and death held carnival.

XIV

  The wintry blast swept wildly o'er the dunes ;
The swiftly changing sands held dangers dire,
So in the fishers' huts the fare was scant,
And strong men, struck with fear, hung up their nets
And laid aside the spear. The housewives sat
No longer in the sun, pillow on knee ;
Bobbins and bones and flaxen thread, which erst
Their busy fingers wove to flowery film,

In shining tangles tasseled the damp walls,
Where seldom smoke or flickering flame arose,
Or savory odors of the steaming food;
While little children, crying in the night,
Hungry and freezing, sobbed their young lives out.
    Ah, me! the darkness of those dismal days! —
The cruel want, the anguish of despair
Through pain and pinching cold and death; — far worse
    worse
Death's pitiless neglect, when death had been
A blessed boon to young and old alike!
And yet, Richberta, all her halls ablaze •
With light and warmth, the crimson and the gold
Superbly sumptuous, as in overflush
Most prodigal of life and all life's needs,
Shimmering and throbbing, in a beauty wild
With an excessive pleasance, counted hers
A hard and bitter lot, demeaned herself
Most shrewishly and sharp, an iron hand
Clinched firmly o'er her treasures, while her maids
And all her ministers besought in vain
Some slight compassion for the starving poor.

XV

Winter at last is ended.
　God be praised for the spring !
Still is the furious tempest ;
　Doubt and despair take wing.
Tenderly lingers the sunshine
　Where the shadows have lain ;
Hope with her smile illumines
　The labors of life again.

Out on the sparkling billows
　The fisherman toils all day,
Homeward at eve returning
　To wife and children gay.
Cold and pain forgotten,
　Though meager and mean their store,
Thankfulness sweetens all things ;
　Plenty is theirs once more.

Yet to the springtime greetings
　Lady Richberta replies
With a gloomy, querulous accent,
　And frowns at the brightening skies.

She is tiring of her vigils,
  And the fair young moon of March
She sees, in the gathering twilight,
  Lighting the stairway arch.

" Of what avail ? " she crieth,
  Yet dares not break her vow,
Slowly ascends the turret,
  And on her knees bends low;
And watch and prayer and penance
  Are offered listlessly;
When, lo! the boon is granted —
  Whitens the purple sea!

XVI

Sunrise shines on the full sails, gleaming
  White as the wings of an angel band;
Wondering whether awake or dreaming,
  Lady Richberta waves her hand.

All its banners the whole fleet, proudly,
  Swift as a lightning's flash, fling wide;
Trumpet and drum to her signal loudly
  Answer across the swelling tide.

Slowly (how slow to her who waits them!)
  The heavily laden ships draw near.
Is it some evil that thus belates them?
  Pales Richberta in mortal fear.

Scarcely the gunwale clears the water;
  Grass grows green on the quarter-deck.
What is this priceless gift they have brought her,
  Holding such mighty force in check?

Who is the old, old man so warily
  Scanning the tide as the ships sail in?
Brave young Heinric Schleyversen!   Verily,
  Perilous voyaging this has been!

XVII

His tall form bowed,
  His visage deeply lined
With many furrows prematurely ploughed,
His yellow beard and hair
Bleached to a snowy whiteness, standing there
  At his proud vessel's prow, the light west wind

Tossing his loose locks, as the helmsman steers
Safely to port amid the welcoming cheers
   Of humble fisher-folk, whom early day
   Calls to the seines that hold their finny prey.
'Tis he — bold Heinric of the eagle eye!
And seeming patriarch of a hundred years.

XVIII

To pale Richberta's cheek a blush goes leaping —
A blush of shame, for conscience is but sleeping —
      So changed is he.
      Her vain decree
   Had not so written in its bond this waste
    Of manhood's prime.
    Life's glory so defaced —
    Degraded — set at nought —
    Appears as her own crime
In this brief moment. Ah! did she but know —
   Could she, so blind, but see
Now is her trial hour! Or weal or woe
   Hangs on the issue of this passing thought,
    To her and thousands more the destiny.

XIX

Scarce had the chapel bells for matins rung
Ere the bold voyagers, every ship in dock,
And all sails furled, were eager to unlade
And to deliver up their precious freight.
Impatiently they wait the admiral's word.

A chosen few at length with him set forth,
Stepping in rhythmic cadence to the notes
Of drum and bugle, resonant and shrill,
With radiant banners waving in the breeze,
Along the busiest streets of Stavoren,
A train of idlers gathering as they go,
While all the bells peal loudly far and near
In joyous greeting of the wealth they bring.

They reach the entrance of the palace courts
Just as the seneschal at noon's high hour
Flings wide the gates, proclaims in haughty tones
That Lady Richberta awaiteth them
In the grand audience hall.

A host of wide-eyed courtiers stand aloof
As in they pass where a magnificence
Of gold and purple, in gay garniture

And garb, hold for a moment's space their gaze —
Those shabby, seaworn men — such contrast sharp
It lends to them and to the gift they bear.

XX

Transcendent loveliness was in the smile
That wreathed Richberta's lips as they advanced,
And through her counselor, Korthar the wise,
She gave them gladsome greeting and loud thanks
For that they had fulfilled her high behest
So faithfully, so well — the while she eyed
Most curiously the clumsy load, that, now,
Each man, obedient to the leader's glance,
Laid at the lady's feet.
                    Thereat he knelt —
Brave Heinric — humbly knelt, and kissed the hem
Of her resplendent robe.   Then, standing, told
In low and modest tones the fearful tale
Of their long voyaging.
                    She heard him not
Save with the outward ear; her mind intent
Upon the treasures lying there and yet

Concealed from view within their rusty sacks,
No eye, no thought has she, for him who speaks
Of icy rigors in the northern seas,
Of blasting noontide heat 'neath tropic suns,
Hunger and pain oft seated at the helm,
While fierce monsoons and pitiless hurricanes
Drave the whole fleet on treacherous rocks, or shoals,
And threatened to engulf in watery graves;
Or base marauders, and vile, savage men,
Devoid of mercy, strove e'en unto death
To wrest the secret of their great emprise;
And how, undaunted still, they kept their way
Those many years.   Yet all a bootless quest,
Until they reached, one quiet autumn day
The long, low beach of a great inland sea,
Whose tranquil tide drew all the ships along,
Like a young brood of swans, far up among
The reeds that fringed with green the little bays,
Which, denting all the coast, a harbor gave
To ships and shallops sent from every clime
That precious thing to gain — the world's best gift —
Abundantly vouchsafed that happy land.

XXI

At those last words he fixed his steadfast gaze
Full on Richberta's wandering eyes, then paused;
Thus drew her thoughts to him as he resumed:
  "A beauteous land, indeed,
Most puissant mistress — beautiful
And grand with all that nature yields!
In quiet pastures herds unnumbered feed;
The hills are white with flocks of softest wool;
  And, in the harvest fields,
Young men and maidens, ruddy as the morn,
Singing for glee, bind up the ripened corn.

"I heard no murmuring of the poor man there
  Of needs left unsupplied,
And no complaining in the busy street
 Of harsh control; but, far and wide,
The peasantry, a hardy, happy race,
Of plainest food had plenty and to spare;
  And, blithe and sweet,
Peace and contentment shone on every face.

"Of flashing gems and gold and velvet stuff,
None did I see.   Mine eyes of those enough,
In all the lands where I had plied my quest,
 Had seen and known ;
 And only now, alone,
Sought out of all earth's products one — the best ;
That which of peace and comfort holds the key;
 Of which whoso deals largess keepeth sway
Of all rebellious hearts, and setteth free
 The abject from their fears ; and day by day,
Dispensing widest trust and love and joy,
Brings for the soul its most approved employ.

 "And so, my liege, I bring
 From that delightsome land,
 As to me seeméd best,
 Of its abundance.   To the water's edge
I filled my ships.   And now in your fair hand
 It is my lofty meed and privilege
To place that wondrous treasure — that best thing."

He ceased.   With skilful fingers quick was loosed
The mouth of one full sack from out the heap

Laid at the lady's feet,
And thence brought forth, from its ungainly keep,
A handful of ripe wheat.

XXII

It was an awful moment.   None dared speak.
Each might then have heard his neighbor's heart beat
In the silence deep
That filled the place while Heinric reverently
Essayed to drop the shining golden grain
Into the lady's ready, outstretched palm.
But with a sudden scorn
Her trembling hand she hastily withdrew,
And every glittering corn
Full on the pavement fell — most sharply fell —
Striking the marble in the ominous calm
With the dull, muffled cadence of a knell.
As with the turn of tide   .
The storm increases, so her accents grew
More and more vehement as her speech found vent
In words her courtiers round grew pale to hear —
Filling the vulgar crowd with horrent fear.

" Her trembling hand she hastily withdrew."　　P. 34.

XXIII

"Thus, minion, thus," she cried,
"Do I cast wide
  You and your palfry freight,
  With my supremest hate.
    This — this you deem,
Base miscreant! the perfectest, the best,
Of all the wealth the wide world can bestow!
    Insolence supreme,
To plan such failure for my highest hope!
That from my splendid scheme would dare to wrest
    Your own conceit so low,
And with my sovereignty essay to cope!

"Presumptuous fool, take quickly hence
Yourself, your crew, and their preposterous load!
And, ere the tide has seven times ebbed and flowed,
    Cast seaward from your ships
Their hateful cargo. If a single grain
    From careless fingers slips
Into a beggar's hand, swift doom — condign —
    The bitterest pain —

Each man shall follow.   Strict obedience
Be yours. — Go! — And from sight most straightly
        place
Of this your luckless errand every trace.''

XXIV

At these last words Korthar raised high his pike,
And prudently waved back the populace,
That gazed with gaping mouths upon the group
Of gallant sailors, crushed so cruelly,
Sadly assuming their despisèd load.
A look of keenest anguish had displaced
The mild benignity that graced so well
The furrowed face of Heinric Schleyversen.
Deeper and darker were the lines now drawn
About his noble features.   Gray as death
The shades contending with the fiery flush
Of injured honor on his lofty brow,
As, tottering feebly, scarcely could he pay
The low obeisance, which, imperiously,
Richberta claimed of all to whom she spake;
While many a gibe and fleer fell on his ear.

And now, again, in jangling dissonance,
The bells with wildest, fiercest tumult fling
Richberta's wrath upon the echoing air
As from her presence slowly he goes forth.

XXV

Wrapped in a purple pall the sun went down.
The eve-star hid her rays.   The hurrying scud,
With wide wings fluttering, hovering, rushing in,
Seemed vast battalions of a ghostly host
Presaging woe.   And when the new moon hung
For a brief space above the city's walls,
She held the old moon in her slender arms,—
Omen most dire ! — at which the fishers' wives
Tended in tears the taper at the pane,
Hushing the children's glee, to hear the steps
Of loved ones hastening home ere bursts the storm.
The white-lipped waves that fiercely lapped the shore
Glowed crimson soon from glare of lamps alight
Through all the harbored fleet.   But wildest scream
Of startled sea gulls seeking safe retreat,
And roar of rampant breakers at the dykes,

Were lost amid the outcries of the crews,—
In their dismay, with frantic turbulence
Working like demons at their desperate task,
Sack upon sack and tierce on tierce, well stored,
From faultless order wresting, with coarse shouts
And oaths, that with the creaking windlass made
Terrific discord.
          At the midnight hour
Out of the bosom of a sable cloud
The north wind burst, with sudden vengeance sped
Throughout the city, raved around the dykes,
Across the dunes, and harried all the port.
The toiling sailors heard it — felt its power
Whistling defiant madness 'mong the shrouds,—
Mast and spar tearing to splinters, crash on crash,
And blow succeeding blow — a hurricane
Indeed,— and yet all stolidly wrought on —
Though, strained in every part, the stout ships reeled —
With deafening uproar striving to outdo
The furious storm.

XXVI

Vainly the admiral
Issued peremptory orders, bidding cease
Their reckless toil.   He knew the jetsam vast —
So many and so many heavy sacks
And tierces numberless — had heaped the shoals,
And rapidly a bar, immense and strong,
Was rearing at the port.   E'en now the tide,
Obstructed thus, raging and roaring sent
A thrill of sharp alarm, chill as stern death,
Through every nerve and vein — a prophecy
Of swift-impending doom.   Such climax near,
More willing he Richberta's ire to dare
Than nature's occult issues to defy.
But all too late his orders.   This alone
Knew they (the reckless crew), or cared to know —
To hide as swiftly as they might beneath
The furious waves their hated freight.   And thus
The livelong night they toiled.   When morning broke,
Rest — a brief space, they took. . . . . .
                              Now, whence and what
The awful change that in the glimmering light

Meets their swift gaze?
                                A flood — a raging flood
Spreads far and wide. . . . .
                                Heinric Schleyversen treads,
From stem to stern, impatiently, the deck
Of his uneasy vessel, uttering low
A groan of deepest anguish, while from all
The watching fleet a cry uprises shrill —
" The dykes ! the dykes are broken ! ". . . .
                                Blank despair,
Or rigid horror, sits on every face
At the wild, widespread ruin. . . . . .

XXVII

                                Springtime rains
And melting snows had swelled the river's tide.
Flevum, full bosomed, aided by the wind,
Had burst triumphantly the barriers strong
That in the ancient days the fathers built
At an uncounted cost of time and toil—
And life (more dear than all), and whose renown
The nation's glory reared, for they had held
In their control the sources of her wealth.

Of this destruction sure, the raging wind,
Its wrath not yet appeased, veered swiftly south,—
The shelving sands along the seashore sent
In rapid eddies, buffeting the waves;
And, mingling there in strange companionship
With wasted cargo of Richberta's fleet —
By rolling surges held and made secure —
Piled rapidly a dune so sharp and sheer
Most vehement current of the inner tide
Might nevermore descend.
                              Yet high and broad
Came on the river, with terrific force,
In its exultant freedom field and fell
Clear sweeping.   And yet on and on it came,
Its rapid waters ravening as they come
Like hungry wolves, around the city's walls
Gnashing their white teeth, till each bulwark fell;
Then, indiscriminate, of hut or hall
Grasping a variant prey, and on its breast
Bearing triumphantly to meet the sea.
Higher and higher the tumultuous waves,
The dune upbuilding, Flevum's trover took,
And with a thunderous roar his progress stayed.

And so the baffled current sullenly
Spread east and west — a restless bay became.
And when the day had fully dawned, behold,
The fleet lay anchored in a wide expanse
Of tossing waters !

XXVIII

Gone were buoy and quay,
All alien vessels, and all kindred craft,
The great storehouses crammed with costly goods,
The mighty derricks, and the fishing gear,
With every fisher's hut, and all the homes
Of thrifty merchants — gone, or hidden deep
Beneath the waves.   Save the one topmost tower
Of proud Richberta's palace, nought was seen
Of stately Stavoren.
The sailors gazed
Aghast.   Where were the gladsome crowds that trod
But yesterday its busy streets? the groups
Of gossips at the cottage doors? and where
The merry children singing songs of spring?
The haughty dame, the flatterers of her court,
And her imperial grandeur?

                              Each for each
Answered in silent language, eye to eye,
Questions unutterable, as still they gazed
In awed amazement and in fearful hope
Some trace, though slight, of sentient life to see
Amid this dreary waste ; when, lo, appears
A white hand beckoning from the turret top !
And whose all knew, and that but yester morn
At this same hour it beckoned last.
                                      Enough !
To crippled mast, or from a broken spar,
A score of men in haste their banners raise,
Tattered and stained with salt sea-spray.
                                      Anon
A white veil flutters from a window bar,
And there the fragile tissue hangs till winds
And waves tear it to shreds.
                              Ay ! day and night
It hung, in mute appeal, as tide on tide
Still higher swelled.   Was that the truce she fain
Would grant the storm-tossed, weary sailors there?
Or sign of keen remorse ? or piteous plea
For pardon of her tyranny ?

God knows,
And He alone; and how, as days went on,
And hunger, pain, and cold the measure filled
Of her imprisonment, she wept and prayed,
Longing for some release.   In her despair,
The one best thing — so scornfully refused —
Seeming, indeed, most priceless gift of earth,
Begged she not humbly, famishing and faint,
That the wild waters bring to her once more,
From the fleet's wasted store of precious wheat,
That handful once despised ?

XXIX

Seven fearful days
Of onset and recoil.   Continuously
The billows surge and leap, their silvery locks
Dashing disheveled 'gainst the trembling tower.
Then came a calm — an ominous, awful calm —
As if the winds and waves, aweary, paused
To gather strength anew ; and in the dark
And solemn midnight watch the sailors heard —
Or fancied so — through the great stillness round,

The *De Profundis* chanted plaintively,
As it had been an angel's voice upraised
From lowest depths of woe.   But, ere it ceased,
Again the storm-wind, its black wings of hail
And biting sleet shook sharp and shrill above
The sleeping waters, and the floods arose,
Raging and booming with terrific force,
And that low voice was hushed — forever hushed ;
While suddenly, all strident with distress,
In gravest bass, antiphonal, the crews
Uplift a *Miserere*, for their ships
No longer own their sway.
                         A plunge — a crash —
A deafening crash, and every keel save one
Asunder parts, and with its gallant crew
Into the ruthless jaws of death soon sinks,
The angered waves thundering defiance fierce.

XXX

And when the gale was spent, the sea at peace,
Heinric Schleyversen in that one ship spared —
Despoiled of sails and spars, a battered hulk —

Beholding the great solitude around —
Not e'en the sheerest pinnacle above the tide —
Called up the remnant of his faithful men ;
With brows uncovered in the golden morn,
From humbled hearts, together poured they forth
Praise and petition to the Power divine
Who holds the sea within His mighty hand.

XXXI

The sun in all his royalty arose,
A smile to nature reconciled cast free —
Blue sky above and laughing waves beneath,
As never storm or sorrow here had birth.
And floating, uncontrolled, before the breeze,
Went the old hulk with Heinric and his crew —
Like Noah in the ark of early time —
Far up and on beyond the city's bounds,
Beyond where Flevum's dykes were once upreared,
Until a haven safe and sure they found.
All perils past, a city there they built
Wherein dwelt peace and plenty evermore.

"And when the gale was spent, the sea at peace."   p. 47.

XXXII

The years, a never-ending flood, roll on.
Long centuries have fled ; and still the tide
Of Flevum's rapid stream flows to the bay,—
The proud blue Zuyder Zee—where yet repose
Beneath the changeful waves the palaces
Of Lady Richberta and all their pomp,
And all the wealth of ancient Stavoren.
Along the shore are many humble homes ;
Here industry and sweet content abide.
And when the wintry snows are drifting high,
And safe in harbor all the fishers' boats—
For furious gales are wrestling with the waves
O'er dune and sandspit — aged crones repeat
(The while their nimble fingers fashion well
Warm hose and garments for the youngster's wear)
To happy children, eager-eyed and keen
For tales of wonder and of perils past,
This legend of Richberta and her doom.
    But when the full-fed urchins, waxing proud,
Coax with cajoling smiles for daintier food,
They tell the story of the babes who died

In want of e'en a crust, till tears fall fast ;
And then, with humble thanks, their daily bread —
The wholesome, healthful loaf of ripened wheat —
Though coarse it be, these wondering little ones
Are glad to take, and with their grandame lift
Their songs of grateful praise to Him who sends
That priceless gift — the world's best thing.

And never Christmas feasting passes by,
If greedy, grasping hands essay to claim
Too large a share of dainties or of toys,
Without a lesson pointed sharp and clear
By brief recall of proud Richberta's sin.

www.ingramcontent.com/pod-product-compliance
Lightning Source LLC
Chambersburg PA
CBHW031930060726
47496CB00008BA/2788